FRIGHTFULLY FUNNY
HALLOWEEN JOKES

UNCLE AMON

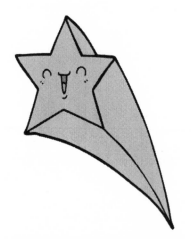

www.UncleAmon.com

ISBN: 9781549747205

TABLE OF CONTENTS

HALLOWEEN JOKES

Q: Did you hear about the girl that wanted to marry a ghost?

A: No one knows what possessed her!

Q: What did the ghost eat for lunch?

A: A booloney sandwich!

Q: What do you say when you meet a monster with sharp teeth?

A: See you later!

Q: How did the hairdresser style the ghost's hair?

A: With a comb and scare dryer!

Q: How does a vampire flirt?

A: She bats her eyes!

Q: How does a vampire enter his house?

A: Through the bat flap!

Q: What do monsters use to stay cool?

A: A scare conditioner!

Q: How does a monster begin a fairy tale?

A: Once upon a slime!

Q: What monster plays the most pranks?

A: Prankenstein!

Q: What does Dracula say to his victims?

A: It has been nice gnawing you!

Q: What kind of monster is safe to put in the washing machine?

A: A wash-n-wear wolf!

Q: Where do monsters like to swim?

A: The Dead Sea!

Q: What is the hardest thing about making monster soup?

A: Stirring it!

Q: What happens if you see twin witches?

A: You cannot tell which witch is which!

Q: What do you do with a green monster?

A: Put it in the sun until it ripens up!

Q: What does a vampire take for a cold?

A: Coffin syrup!

Q: What is Dracula's favorite flavor of ice cream?

A: Vein-illa!

Q: How do you address a werewolf?

A: Very politely and from far away!

Q: What does a mother monster say to her kids at dinnertime?

A: Do not talk with someone in your mouth!

Q: Where do children ghosts go during the day?

A: Day-scare centers!

Q: Why was the monster standing on his head?

A: He was turning things over in his mind!

Q: What do you call a smart monster?

A: Frank Einstein!

Q: Why are vampire families so close?

A: Because blood is thicker than water!

Q: Why is Hollywood full of vampires?

A: They need someone to play the bit parts!

Q: Did you hear about the vampire who got married?

A: He proposed to his goulfriend!

Q: What did Frankenstein's ear say to the other?

A: I had no clue we lived on the same block!

Q: What Central American country has the most haunted houses?

A: Ghosta Rica!

Q: Where is Dracula's office?

A: The Vampire State Building!

Q: How do ghosts travel?

A: On a scareplane!

Q: Why was the vampire easy to fool?

A: Because he was a complete sucker!

Q: What does a vampire stand on after taking a shower?

A: A bat mat!

Q: How come ghosts do not make good magicians?

A: You can see right through their tricks!

Q: What kind of witch loves the beach?

A: A sandwitch!

Q: What do you call two witches that share a room?

A: Broom-mates!

Q: Where do monsters get their hair done?

A: The ugly parlor!

Q: What do you get if you cross a vampire and a mummy?

A: Something scary you would not want to unwrap!

Q: What did the werewolf write at the bottom of his letter?

A: Best vicious!

Q: What does a monster say when he meets you for the first time?

A: Pleased to eat you!

Q: What is a vampire's favorite fruit?

A: Blood oranges!

Q: What kind of book do monsters like to read?

A: One with a cemetery plot!

Q: What is a vampire's favorite drink?

A: A bloody Mary!

Q: What did the mother ghost say to the baby ghost?

A: Only spook when your spooken to!

Q: What does an Australian witch ride on?

A: A broomerang!

Q: On which day do monsters eat people?

A: Chewsday!

Q: What is every young monster's favorite amusement park ride?

A: The scary-go-round!

Q: What did the teenage witch ask her parents?

A: May I have the keys to the broom tonight?

Q: How do you stop a monster from digging up your garden?

A: Take away his shovel!

Q: What city do ghosts like the most?

A: Mali-Boo!

Q: What do ghosts drink in the morning?

A: Coffee with two screams and a sugar!

Q: Where did the monster keep his extra pair of hands?

A: In a handbag!

Q: What would you get if you crossed and a famous movie director?

A: Steven Spellberg!

Q: Why did the vampire take up acting?

A: It was in his blood!

Q: What happened to the monster that put his false teeth in backwards?

A: He ate himself!

Q: What is Dracula's favorite fruit?

A: Neck-tarines!

Q: What do you get when you cross Bambi with a ghost?

A: Bamboo!

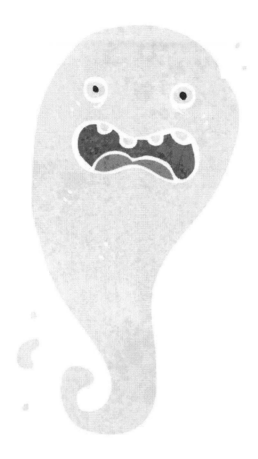

Q: What did the vampire do to stop his son from biting his nails?

A: He cut all his fingers off!

Q: What do you get if you cross a vampire and a circus entertainer?

A: Someone that goes straight for the juggler!

Q: How do witches lose weight?

A: They join weight witches!

Q: How do witches keep their hair in place?

A: Scare spray!

Q: Why did Frankenstein squeeze his girlfriend to death?

A: He had a crush on her!

Q: Where do you find monster boogers?

A: On the end of a monster's fingers!

Q: What is Dracula's car called?

A: The mobile blood unit!

Q: What kind of car did the Frankenstein buy?

A: A monster truck!

Q: What is Dracula's favorite pudding?

A: Leeches and scream!

Q: Why doesn't Dracula have any friends?

A: Because he's a pain in the neck!

Q: Did you hear about the vampire that died of a broken heart?

A: He had loved in vein!

Q: How does Dracula like his food served?

A: Bite-sized pieces!

Q: How can you tell if a monster has a glass eye?

A: It comes out in conversation!

Q: What can a monster do that you can't?

A: Count to 25 on his fingers!

Q: How do you stop a monster from smelling?

A: Cut off his nose!

Q: Why did the ghost go to the amusement park?

A: He wanted to ride a roller ghoster!

Q: What do vampires have every morning?

A: A coffin break!

Q: Why did the student witch make bad grades in school?

A: She could not spell properly!

Q: What is the best way to talk to a vampire?

A: From long distance!

Q: What kind of street does a zombie like best?

A: A dead end!

Q: Why are haunted houses so noisy in April?

A: That is when the ghosts do their spring screaming!

Q: How do vampires sail the sea?

A: In blood vessels!

Q: What is a witch's favorite TV show?

A: Lifestyles of the Witch and Famous!

Q: What is served for lunch at Monster School?

A: Human beans, boiled legs, and eyes-cream!

Q: What directions did the ghost give to the goblin?

A: Make a fright turn at the corner!

Q: Where do ghosts get their mail?

A: The ghost office!

Q: When do vampires bite?

A: On Wincedays!

Q: What does a monster do when he loses his head?

A: He calls a head hunter!

Q: What did the police officer say about the mummy murder case?

A: It is time to wrap it up!

Q: Which ghost ate too much porridge?

A: Ghouldilocks!

Q: What vampire loves sweets?

A: Count Snackula!

Q: How is a ghost like an empty house?

A: Because there's no body there!

Q: What do you get if you cross Dracula with knight?

A: A bite in shining armor!

Q: Did you hear about the ghost comedian?

A: He was booed off stage!

Q: When do ghosts play tricks on each other?

A: April Ghoul's Day!

Q: Which day of the week do ghosts like best?

A: Moandays!

Q: What do sea monsters like to snack on?

A: Fish and ships!

Q: What should you do if a monster runs through your front door?

A: Run through the back door!

Q: What is a ghost's favorite play?

A: Romeo and Ghouliet!

Q: What is big, furry, dangerous, and has wheels?

A: A monster on roller-skates!

Q: What is the first thing that vampires learn in school?

A: The alphabat!

Q: What do you get if you cross a monster with a flea?

A: A lot of scared dogs!

Q: What is big and hairy and goes beep, beep, beep?

A: A monster in a traffic jam!

FIND THE DIFFERENCES

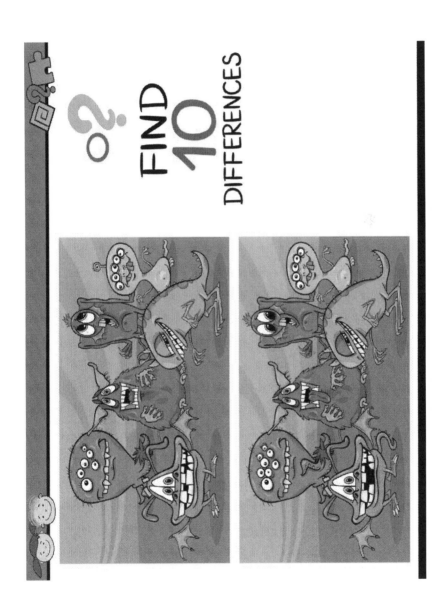

MAZE 1

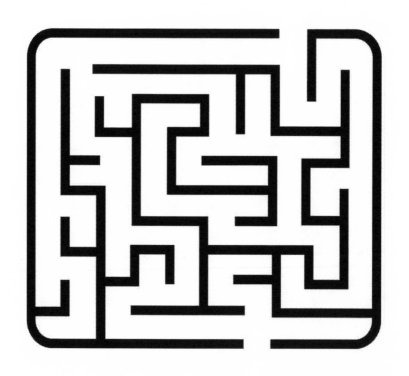

MAZE 2

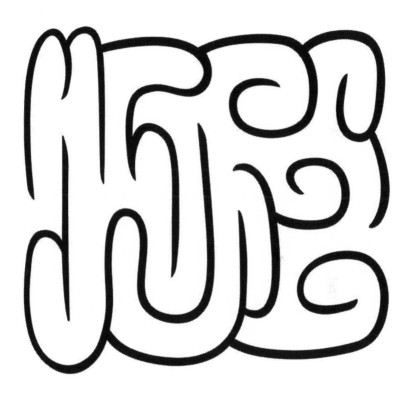

MAZE 3

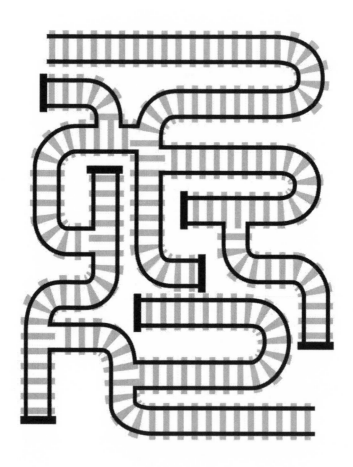

MAZE 4

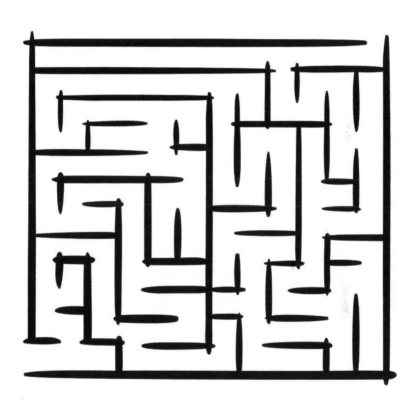

SOLUTIONS

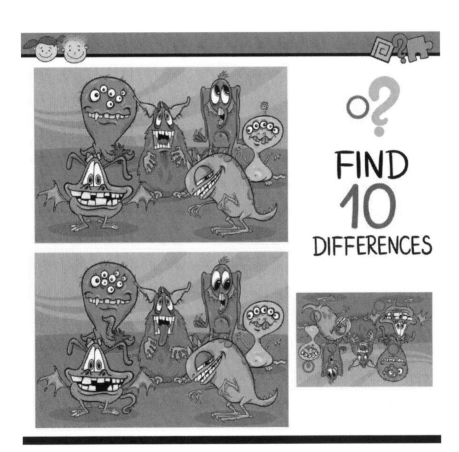

FIND
10
DIFFERENCES

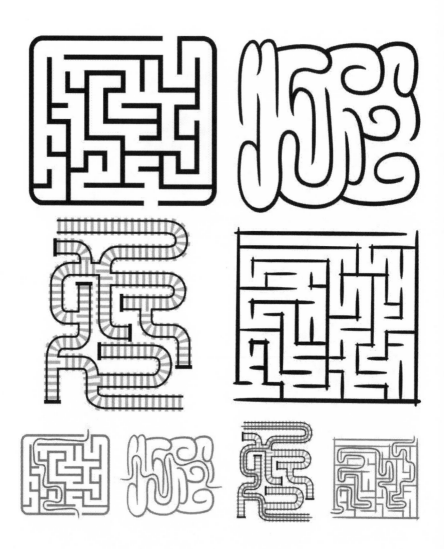

ABOUT THE AUTHOR

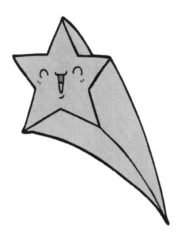

Uncle Amon began his career with a vision. It was to influence and create a positive change in the world through children's books by sharing fun and inspiring stories.

Whether it is an important lesson or just creating laughs, Uncle Amon provides insightful stories that are sure to bring a smile to your face! His unique style and creativity stand out from other children's book authors, because he uses real life experiences to tell a tale of imagination and adventure.

"I always shoot for the moon. And if I miss? I'll land in the stars." -Uncle Amon

For more fun books by Uncle Amon, please visit:

www.UncleAmon.com/books

Made in the
USA
Middletown, DE